THE
"TERRIBLE"
BULLIES

www.mascotbooks.com

The Terrible Bullies

For more information, please contact:
Mascot Books
620 Herndon Parkway, Suite 320
Herndon, VA 20170
info@mascotbooks.com

Library of Congress Control Number: 2020905908

CPSIA Code: PRV0720A
ISBN-13: 978-1-64543-485-6

Printed in the United States

I dedicate this book to my friend and tutor Mr. David Chappell of Literary Legacies. He was the one who got me started on my first book and discovered that I have this creative writing talent.

If it weren't for him, I would not have been on this journey right now with my writing skills as a teen author. Thank you.

THE "TERRIBLE" BULLIES

RIYANI PATEL

ILLUSTRATED BY
SHAWN DSOUZA

Foreword

About two years ago, I hosted a book reading where a young author read a few chapters of her new book to a local children's group. The reading and the prose were absolutely fantastic and were absorbed by children like sweet ice cream on a hot Sunday afternoon. The author (and reader) was Riyani Patel, and her reading was the true spirit of inspiration.

Riyani—only thirteen years old at the time—dazzled, intrigued, and inspired the audience, both young and old, with her character, presence, likability, and calming maturity. I personally was dazzled by her control of the prose, her endearing delivery style, and the uncanny way she conveyed her words to the listeners. I listened in awe, and I trembled inside. I knew this young author battles Tourette's syndrome and my nerves feared that a might spoil the entire atmosphere.

The reading began as entertaining, soon turned to amazing, and ended in pure inspiration for everyone present. Riyani demonstrated to the group that not only is she going to blossom into a great author, she is already a great model and inspiration to all that must overcome. The period should go on the inside of the quotation mark.

Also, I worry that the quotation marks bring a negative connotation. In other words, through her actions, resilience, perseverance, and writings, Riyani will inspire all of us to be a super hero just like herself and to put fear aside.

Congratulations to Riyani, on all fronts, including the publishing of this second book, which is as fantastic as her first book.

The messages conveyed by the young author of *The "Terrible" Bullies* are inspiring in both meaning and in pure, unfiltered substance. In her second publication, Riyani expands on the trials, the resolve, and the virtues that young readers perpetually encounter throughout their lives.

Without doubt, young readers will be attracted to this story at many levels. Riyani communicates to her audience how to deal with the antagonists of life. Almost more importantly, she comforts her audience with the message that antagonists will be on stage with you all your life—and that's okay.

As we quickly learn in Riyani's writing, bullies—friends and family members—can and will be, at times, one in the same. Understanding how to properly handle both the antagonist and the circumstance properly is clearly expert to Riyani and expert in how she educates all of us in her writings.

As a parent and an older reader of Riyani's books, I must say that the story and respective messages of this book resonate soundly with all ages. We never really stop learning how to cope with life's struggles as we grow, and this book reminds us that struggles never really go away. I'm sure everyone has felt at some point that the whole world might seem like a bully at times. Learning to neutralize, understand, and accept that bully or that circumstance is the best we can do and while continuing to stay vigilante as life progresses.

This book warmly reminds and guides us through the tales of ordinary young people experiencing timeless troubles and maturing into ordinary heroes.

Riyani Patel has conquered Tourette's syndrome, which she will live with her entire life. I personally would never had known that Riyani has Tourette's, which is a testament to her strength and resolve. She not only inspires others with Tourette's—she authors heroism.

Marty Kacin

2020

Marty Kacin is a Silicon Valley Visionary, Technologist, and the founder of the Los Altos Research Center. Marty is the father of TheMatrix™, a new Internet computing platform that hopes to drive a whole new, rational, and privacy-friendly technology industry.

IN HER OWN WORDS

Hi, everyone. Thanks for taking the time to read this book and putting your cell phones down. It is a fun and easy read that I hope you enjoy. Having been bullied myself because of my vocal and motor tics from Tourette's, I know what it is like to be teased, hurt, and embarrassed.

I have three messages to share about this book. The first message is for the person who is being bullied: You should have courage and stick up for yourself. I know it is hard, but it is the right thing to do. You don't have to be scared or afraid of anyone.

The second message is for the person who is the bully: Whatever you say or do, you should know that your words and actions are harmful to others. Have the awareness to be kind to others. You should want to be the better person.

And last, but not least, the third message: The word "terrible" is in quotations in the title because the story may reveal why bullies aren't so bad after all.

First Day of High School

It is a Thursday, which marks the start of ninth grade. Tanya is super excited to go back to school, but she is also sad because she doesn't want summer to end. Tanya dresses up cute for the first day at her new school. Her school is about fifteen minutes away, so it is not too bad. When Tanya arrives, she sees a huge building with lots of kids. Tanya becomes even more excited to see her friends and Jake.

Within one second, Tanya screams, "OMG!" She runs up to her friends and babbles with them about summer, the places she visited, etc. A few minutes later, Tanya spots Jake and runs up to him to give him a very big hug. They talk about summer, how much they have both changed, where they went, and what they wanted to do but could not because how busy their summer was.

Later in the day, Tanya is instructed by the teacher on the syllabus of what the expectations are for school. Fourth period comes around, and Tanya receives a syllabus by her teacher on what the P.E. rules are. Tanya also learns how to open her school locker, as well as her P.E. locker. The best part is that Tanya's friends are mostly in all of her classes, so she is not left out. The sad part is that Jake is not in any of her classes, but they will still hang out with each other during brunch and lunch.

When school is over, her dad comes to pick her up. He energetically asks Tanya, "Hey, honey, how was your first day of school?"

Tanya is so excited to talk about her day, and she bursts out all the things she had fun with that day: seeing friends in her classes, getting to see Jake in the hall, and her teachers seeming pretty nice.

"High school is not as scary as I thought it would be!" Tanya says excitedly to her father on the car ride home.

When they arrive home, her mom, Karen, and her dog, Zoozoo, are waiting outside of their house.

Karen picks up Zoozoo and walks up to Tanya and asks, "Hey, honey, how was your first day of school?"

Tanya responds with, "It was great! I had so much fun!" Tanya picks up Zoozoo and says, "I missed you so much, my little pumpkin!"

Since today was the first day of school, Tanya does not have homework, but she has to get her syllabi signed by her parents. That is the first thing she takes care of, so she can have free time to do anything she wants to do. Tanya plays with her dog for a bit, and then she goes to the park with her friends. They have a carpool with one of her friend's parents who comes along and picks them all up. They are all neighbors, so it is always easy to pick them all up in one go.

After their trip to the park, they go to a gas station called Phil's Gas.

They pick up some snacks and head to her friend Serena's place after that. They hang out for a bit until it is nighttime and dinner time. The carpool drops Tanya and her other friends back at their houses.

At home, Tanya has rice noodles for dinner. At night, she does her normal routine that she has been doing since the last school year. Tanya gets ready for bed, and she thinks about how her next day of school is going to be.

Diamond Comes To School

It's Friday, and it's Tanya's second day of school. She gets ready, looking at herself in the mirror and feels pretty, wearing white jeans and a black flannel with her hair straightened. She packs her lunch and goes to school. Tanya does not go by herself, though, as she goes with her best friends since most of them live in the same neighborhood as her. The fifteen minutes goes by with them chatting, listening to their music, and more young people things.

Once they arrive at school, they still have time before the warning bell rings to go to class, so they walk around and explore what they haven't seen at school. Tanya notices a face similar to Diamond's face. Tanya freaks out a bit and says, "Oh, God! That's Diamond!" She screams it so loud, and Diamond hears.

Diamond walks up to Tanya and says, "Am I really that scary to you? I haven't even done anything to you since last school year. It's only the second day of school."

Diamond walks away, and Tanya is still in shock that Diamond doesn't scream at her or do anything bad to her.

Tanya says to herself, "I shouldn't have screamed that."

Just then, the bell rings, and they all scurry to class. Tanya's first period is history. She still feels bad that she said that to Diamond, but then twenty minutes later, she gets over it. The rest of her day flies by with her being responsible and turning in all her syllabi, as well as getting her work done.

At the end of the day, Tanya goes home after school. Tanya tells her parents that school was okay for her today. She tells them about what she said to Diamond that made her feel bad and how she is scared. When Tanya is scared of something, she has to say it out loud so that people can actually hear her.

Tanya's parents reassure her that it's okay, and that everything will be fine. Her mom says, "Who knows if Diamond has changed over the summer or not."

Her dad joins the conversation and says, "Well, you won't see her that often since it's high school, and there are lots of kids."

Tanya says, "True, true . . ."

Her mom then says, "Your food will make you happy since it's a vegetarian quesadilla! Your favorite!"

An excited Tanya responds, "Oh, heck yeah! Let's eat!"

Once they're done eating, Tanya does her normal routine for nighttime and goes to bed confident that she will not have a bad third day at school.

Tanya and Jake's First High School Date

It is a Saturday morning, and Tanya wakes up super early at around 7:30 a.m. This is because it is her first ever high school date with Jake! She doesn't have to shower because, in her usual routine, she showers at night. She is wearing skinny white jeans with a black top and a jean jacket. Her hair is not straightened, so she decides to put her hair up in a high ponytail. She puts on some makeup, and the last step is to put on her favorite pair of boots from her favorite brand called Boot Addicts. Once Tanya is all ready, she is just in time because she is done at 8:30 a.m. She has to leave with Jake by 8:45 a.m.

Her date is not only with Jake, because Jake's cousin named Noah comes, too, with his girlfriend named Alyssa. They are going on a double date. They go to a breakfast place called The Liyu, where they have so many varieties of food. They all decide to share one meal, which is called the "8 Stacks of Heaven." The meal consists of eight really big pancakes with bowls of butter, syrup, strawberries, whipped cream, and powdered sugar. It is an expensive $16, but the total adds up to $24 because all four of them order a $2 drink.

When they are done eating, they split the check so all four of them pay $6 each. They enjoy their breakfast, and then they go to Tanya's house to drop Tanya off. Jake comes into Tanya's house, and Tanya says with a smiling face, "Jake, thank you so much for this double date. I had lots of fun. Thanks for making it a really good time for me."

Tanya gives Jake a very tight hug and then says goodbye as he leaves the house. As she closes the door, she thinks about the first time she saw him last year and dreamed about how magical it would be to go on a date with him. Her dream finally came true.

The rest of Tanya's day goes by. She invites her friends over to do crafts with her, runs errands with her mom and dad, and goes to parties. When Tanya goes home, she is super tired and does not feel like doing her nightly routine, so she just goes to sleep with Zoozoo.

Rumors About New High School Students

When Tanya arrives at school on Monday, her friends look scared. Tanya asks, "Oh jeez . . . what's wrong?"

Tanya's friends respond with, "We've been hearing that kids from Minneapolis are coming to our suburban school. Minneapolis people are tough."

Tanya becomes scared because she had a bad experience with people from Minneapolis. When her cousins from Minneapolis came over when she was six years old, they teased her. They teased Tanya with comments such as, "You are an only child! You don't have anybody to be here with you! You dress funny! Be cool like us instead of playing with unicorn stuffed animals, baby dolls, and tea party sets! You're nothing but a spoiled brat!"

Tanya stared at the ground and starts tearing up because of this experience.

Her friends ask her, "What's wrong!?"

Tanya explains this to her friends, and they feel bad for her. They start telling her nice things, and Tanya feels a bit better. Throughout the day, Serena and Crystal take Tanya to an empty spot at the school where no one really goes, and they tell her, "Since the bullies are here and you had an experience with this, we will invite our other friends and eat lunch here."

"We will also stay here when it's brunch time, too," replies Crystal.

Tanya thinks, *It's a good idea, but if we stay here all the time, it would be boring, because it's just grass, concrete, and fields.*

Tanya replies back with her thoughts and tells her friends, "We have to be brave!"

Serena says, "True that, because you were brave fighting Diamond last year!"

They all walk back to the school campus and head to their classes.

As Tanya starts with her first class, which is history, they do the Pledge of Allegiance and warm-ups, an exercise where the teacher writes a question on the board and the students have to answer them. After that is done, it is time for the new kids to make the announcements introducing themselves to their new classmates. The first kid starts by saying, "Hi, my name is Raphael. I am fifteen years old, and I am adventurous."

"Hi, my name is Adele, and I am fifteen, as well. I like to hang out with friends."

"Hi, my name is Carlos. I came to this city with my family four years ago. This is a very interesting school."

"My name is Ivanna. I am Carlos' younger sister."

"Hello, my name is Riku. I look forward to a new environment. And I volunteer at a nursing home."

Tanya loves her school because of how many international kids transfer to this school. Their families move here because of the great school district and affordable housing, so it is a perfect place for international families to come to when they first move to America. Tanya thinks it makes her school special.

"What's up, people? I am Kiana Weeks, and I like to bake. I actually have a cousin who is in this class. I am sure she recognized my voice when I first spoke! Hey Tanya—I'm baaaaaack."

Everyone stares at Tanya, and she is surprised. She didn't know this was coming. Throughout the day before lunch time, Tanya feels nervous to meet her cousin since she hasn't met up with her since childhood. Tanya looks shocked and glances at her friends, saying, "That was the cousin I was talking about who bullied me when I was in Washington."

At that moment, Tanya's cell phone rings. Before saying hello, there is a voice saying, "Meet me by the track and field bathrooms. Come by yourself. Don't bring anyone with you."

Tanya says, "I have to leave. No one come with me!"

Tanya starts walking to the track and field bathrooms. When she arrives, she sees her cousin. Kiana gives her a confident hug, but Tanya gives a nervous hug. They start talking about why Kiana and her friends moved into the city. Kiana replies, "You don't need to know about that." They talk about life and what they have done for the last few years. Lunch is now over. Throughout the rest of the school day, Tanya is nervous about what's going to happen with her because she knows Kiana is a mean person.

Unwelcomed Surprise

When Tanya gets picked up from school that Monday afternoon, she grows irritated with her mom. Karen asks, "How was school? Are you okay? You look a bit disappointed."

Tanya replies, "I am disappointed. With you, though . . ."

Karen asks, "With me!? Why?"

Tanya angrily responds, "You knew Kiana was coming to Bridge Bank High School, and you never told me this . . . why didn't you?"

Karen confesses, "It was a surprise, though. I just wanted you to be happy."

Tanya says, "You expect me to be happy with Kiana? Do you realize what she did to me back in Washington, D.C.?!"

Karen replies, "Oh sweetie, it's been eight years since we lived there! I'm sure Kiana has changed."

Tanya laughs sarcastically and says, "Yeah, Mom. You don't know what Kiana has done." Tanya breaks down into tears and starts crying. "She treated me horribly. She used to hit me, she broke my tea party set and blamed it on me, and you started yelling at me. She said really mean and nasty things to me." Tanya starts crying even more. Tanya says, "Mom, you don't get it. Kiana was acting innocent when we were in Washington, and she blamed me for breaking the tea party set. I loved that tea party set. I would never break it because it was one hundred forty-five dollars. Now that Kiana is here, she is being mean again. She has a bunch of her mean, bully friends! Tell me, Mom, what do you think of Kiana? Do you think she actually changed?"

Karen is speechless for a minute and then says, "I'm very sorry, sweetheart. I didn't realize until you told me this. Tell me more when we go inside the house. We're almost home."

When they get to the house, Tanya starts telling stories to both her mom and dad. Tanya's dad knew Kiana was coming to Tanya's high school, too.

"I don't know what I am going to do tomorrow," says Tanya.

Karen says, "Tanya, don't worry about tomorrow. Focus on today."

"Fine. I'll just do my homework," replies Tanya.

The rest of the day goes by with Tanya doing her homework, taking Zoozoo for a walk, talking to her friends about this whole situation, and completing her nightly routine. Tanya goes to bed worried about the whole incident.

The Bullying Starts

Tanya arrives at school the next morning, and she sees Riku bullying other students. She walks out of her car immediately and nicely says, "Hey! Please stop bullying other kids, Riku. It's not nice, and you don't know what they are going through."

Riku's facial expression turns to rolled eyes and raised eyebrows. He responds, "You can't tell me what to do, sweetheart."

Tanya wears a disgusted look on her face and says, "Um, okay, don't ever call me that again," and she walks away with dignity.

Tanya observes more bullying walking to her first period class. The bullies are Raphael and Adele this time. She catches the two pushing other kids, talking trash in French, and laughing about it. When they realize that Tanya is looking at them, Raphael and Adele ask Tanya, "What? Do you have a problem with us? If you do, say it to our face! We are not scared."

Tanya has a mad look on her face and responds, "No! I don't have any problem with you, but what you are doing is wrong!" She walks away fast so that they can't catch up to her.

Tanya sees an incident that startles her not long after: It is Ivanna and Carlos bullying Diamond! Ivanna tells Diamond, "Just because you're a cheerleader doesn't mean that you're pretty. To be honest, you're kind of ugly!" Carlos and Ivanna start laughing, and Carlos pulls Diamond's hair.

Diamond starts crying and exclaims, "Please stop! PLEASE!"

Carlos and Ivanna ignore her, and they start laughing even more.

Tanya yells, "Hey! Do you think that's appropriate? Do you think that's kind?"

Before Tanya can say one more thing, Ivanna says, "Shut up!" She pulls Tanya's hair before walking into class.

Diamond looks shocked because Tanya defended her. Diamond says, "Thank you so much, Tanya! I didn't even expect this. I was just walking, and they came up to me and talked trash. They treated me horribly."

"Yeah, no problem." Tanya doesn't realize that the bell rang, and she says, "I have to go. Bye, Diamond." Tanya speed-walks to her class to try and make it on time. When she arrives to her class, Tanya receives a tardy, and she has to stay for a few minutes in the classroom during brunch time when class is over.

Tanya explains what happened to her English teacher, Mrs. Cathy Carter, during her tardy detention. Tanya explains what she witnessed, and her teacher is shocked because the school has a policy against bullying.

Mrs. Carter says, "Thanks for telling me all of this, Tanya. I will definitely report this kind of behavior to the principal's office."

After all of these incidents, Tanya finally goes home, and she tells her mom and dad what happened. They have a shocked facial expression.

They both say, "Oh, God, this is not right!"

Karen says, "Was Kiana involved in this, too?"

Tanya responds, "No, no, no, I didn't see Kiana bullying anyone. I'm glad, though."

Then after the discussion is over, Tanya does her daily routine.

Tanya is just about to fall asleep when she receives a message on Snapchat. "Diamond.408 added you as a friend!" Tanya thinks, *Why would Diamond want to add me on Snapchat?*

Tanya adds Diamond anyway. Right after Tanya adds her, Diamond calls. Tanya picks up her phone and starts talking to her. Diamond is being very nice and says, "OMG! Thank you so much for defending me this morning. How can I ever repay you?"

"Oh, no problem! It was the right thing to do. Bullying isn't right at all," says Tanya.

Diamond wants to talk some more, but Tanya has to go to sleep as it is getting late.

The Family Reunion

On Saturday evening, it is the family reunion. Tanya has to go with her parents. The reunion is held a fancy house that is eight thousand square feet big. When Tanya walks in, she sees so many people that she has to reunite with. Fifteen minutes go by, and Tanya doesn't expect to see what she sees. It is Diamond, who is at the family reunion, too!

Tanya says, "Hey, Diamond, whatcha doing here? Do you have any relatives here?"

Diamond replies, "OMG, Tanya! What are YOU doing here!? It's so good to see you!" Diamond continues, "Oh yeah, that's my grandma right there."

Tanya replies, "And that's my grandma talking to your grandma."

Both of the grandmothers look over at Tanya and Diamond.

The grandmothers say, "Oh yeah, we are cousins!"

Tanya and Diamond swoop their heads so fast that their necks crack a bit, but they don't care.

They two girls yell in an excited voice at the same time, "So that means we are also cousins!"

They scream so loud, prompting the majority of people in the same living room as them to look shocked. Diamond reminisces about the past and about what happened between her and Tanya. Diamond thinks it's a good idea to apologize to Tanya.

Diamond says, "Hey, Tanya. I need to talk to you privately, so let's go into a room where it's quiet."

Tanya responds, "Okay."

The two head upstairs and go into the guest bedroom. They both sit down, and Diamond starts sobbing. Diamond says, "OMG I'm so, so sorry that I bullied you in eighth grade. I don't know what was wrong with me. I am a horrible person."

Tanya starts crying, too, and says, "No, no, no, don't cry. You are not a horrible person. I forgot about that until you reminded me, and I forgive you."

They both give each other a very long hug. Diamond says, "I don't know why I bullied you so much in eighth grade. You never did anything wrong to me, but you don't know the full truth, which I am about to tell you. The truth is, I was bullied in elementary school, and it made me so upset. I wanted to seem as cool as the bullies. I wanted to bully other people. I didn't want to be that kid who got bullied, so that's the truth. I bullied you. I'm sorry."

Tanya has a shocked look on her face and says, "OMG, all of this happened to you, so you became a bully?"

Diamond tears up, but Tanya says, "No, no, no, don't cry. Let's forget about the past and move forward. I totally forgive you. It's okay, and I understand."

They give each other another hug and then head downstairs. After that, they both enjoy the dancing, food, and reuniting with relatives they haven't seen in a long time. After that, they all go home.

Information About The Bullies

It is a Sunday morning, and Tanya and Diamond have a plan. Their plan is to expose the bullies. They talk about it, and they want to include Jake, as well. They make a group chat through text, and it is just the three of them. Tanya texts, "What are their intentions, though, and how can we dig up info?"

Jake replies, "We can be mini-detectives and ask the police what they are allowed to tell us about them."

Diamond and Tanya respond with, "That's a great idea!"

They don't want to do the investigating right away. They need a couple of days to create a slideshow to expose them. Their idea is to talk about all six bullies and all the mean and negative things they have done to them and other students. And especially for Tanya, who wants to add a slide that describes the vocal and motor tics that she was bullied for in the first place. Their goal is to present the slideshow on Wednesday in the school gym in front of all the students and staff at Bridge Bank High. They all decide to go to Minneapolis that day.

They ask their parents, and they all say yes. All of them are busy except for Diamond's dad, so he drops them off. The police station in the city is forty-five minutes away from their homes. They all go in, except for Diamond's dad, because he is waiting in the car. They ask the police officers questions about the bullies, and they even brought a little notepad and a pencil to take notes. They asked if they did bad things, if they stole, and if they ever lied. Surprisingly, all of the answers were, "Yes."

Diamond's dad calls and wants to know if they are done investigating because he is growing worried. Diamond opens the car door and laughs, saying, "Yes!"

On the way back home, there is traffic. Diamond's dad asks, "So, what did you guys find out?

The trio explain what the police officers told them.

Diamond's dad says, "Good grief! Kids these days!"

Jake says, "Yup."

Diamond and Tanya received similar information to Jake's, but they don't want to reveal it just yet.

Traffic has gone down, and they arrive home really fast. After that, Tanya has to run a few errands with her mom and dad. They get back home kind of late at 6:30 p.m. Even though she is tired, Tanya does her routine since she started in the eighth grade. After that, Tanya goes to bed and is ready to find out more information the next day.

Information About The New Bullies
Part Two

It is Monday morning, but Tanya doesn't go to school. She stays home because she has a painful stomach ache, and she threw up multiple times in the middle of the night. Tanya texts Diamond and Jake saying, "Hey, I won't be able to make it to school, but I will be able to come with you guys after school to the juvenile hall."

They both text back, "Aww! Feel better! See ya then!"

Tanya reads their text and goes to sleep. Later, she doesn't get too dolled up, but she wears something relaxing. The plan is for her to get dressed, and Diamond's dad is picking the three of them up after school. Diamond's dad comes to pick up Tanya, and she grabs her little notepad to take notes to gather more information.

The juvenile hall is just twenty-five minutes away, and it is not in the city. After they arrive, Diamond's dad waits in the car again. The trio goes inside, and they have to get checked before they can go past security. They get checked by security and walk in. The police officers tell Tanya, Diamond, and Jake that the troublesome kids committed petty theft, like stealing groceries, money, and clothes. The police officer was a bit surprised to learn that one of the kids stole medicine.

Jake, Tanya, and Diamond are very shocked and say, "Wow, thanks so much for telling us this. We never knew how other teenagers could behave like this."

The police officers say, "Yeah, no problem. If you guys need any more information, let us know. Here is the number for the facility."

All of them say, "Thanks so much!"

On the way home, they all agree to one thing, which is Diamond's idea. She says, "Do you guys really want to go to the courthouse? I mean, we got a lot of information we need already. Going there is just gonna be too much."

Tanya and Jake respond, "Yeah that's true. So, we don't have to go to court tomorrow. What we can do is put up the slideshow tomorrow at the assembly."

Jake says, "Let's just go home already."

After a long day, they all go home.

Plotting Revenge

The next Tuesday, the trio ask their parents if they can take a day off to work on the slideshow. All of their parents grant them permission, as long as they are catching up with schoolwork online and are emailing their teachers about missing work. They all say, "You got it!"

They all decide to meet at Coffee Cup, a local café. They all walk because the café is just five minutes away. They all bring their computers, notes, and phones. They sit inside because it is a bit chilly out. They divide their work into six slides, so each person has two slides to create.

Diamond says, "I'll make the slides about Carlos and Ivanna."

Jake says, "I'll do Adele and Raphael."

Last but not least, Tanya says, "I got Riku and Kiana."

They spend the rest of the morning finishing up the final slides, putting up videos, and making small edits so the slides are perfect to present the next day. While working, they all take money so that they can buy something to eat and drink. When they are done, they all head back to Diamond's house to hang out, do some schoolwork, and watch movies.

The rest of the day goes by so quickly, and Tanya does her normal routine and goes to bed, ready and prepared to present tomorrow.

Confronting the Bullies

It is the next morning and time to go to school. It is also the day for the trio to expose the bullies. Everyone gets ready, packs their lunches, and heads off to school. The assembly starts at 10:45 a.m., but what the teachers don't know is that it's an "exposing bullies" assembly.

Jake tells the teachers that it is an assembly for "How to Respect the School." But that's not it at all. After one of the teachers tells all the students to settle down and be quiet, they begin their presentation.

Diamond is up first. She says to the audience, "I've got to tell you something about Ivanna and Carlos, and it is not a good something. They used to live in a bad environment where they pick pocketed people, got into fights at school, and bullied other students."

The teachers look at each other and realize this isn't the "Respect the School" presentation. The students' jaws drop, and Ivanna and Carlos appear so mad and a bit embarrassed at the same time.

It is Jake's turn, and he says, "Oh, I have something very sweet to say about Adele and Raphael . . . haha, yeah right! No, I have some bad secrets to share about these two. Both of them scammed people, painted graffiti on walls, got caught watching drag racing, and bullied kids in school."

Now the teachers look so mad at the trio because they lied to them. The students in the assembly started to scream, "OMG! Wow, is this really true?!"

Adele and Raphael look so embarrassed and upset at the same time. Students are giving dirty looks and throwing stuff at them. Students are saying, "How does it feel now? Getting stuff thrown at you guys."

Tanya speaks into the microphone, "Okay, okay, everyone! The assembly is not over yet, so everyone please just settle down." Everyone gets quiet. Tanya says, "Now it's Riku's turn! Riku lived in a non-friendly, suburban neighborhood. He stole money and certain types of medicine."

Everyone is like, "OMG! That is super crazy!"

Riku's face turned as red as a tomato. He wants to say something, but he doesn't. Tanya then says, "I'm not done yet! I saved the best for last! The last bully I'm gonna talk about is my own cousin, Kiana Weeks. Some people may not know, but Kiana is my cousin. She didn't steal anything, but she used to bully me when I was a little girl. She broke my very expensive tea party set, which was one hundred forty-five dollars. She put the blame on me, saying that I broke it. Also, she used to call me a spoiled brat. She threw my stuffed animals at me, and one time she threw a stuffed animal so hard at me that my nose started to bleed."

Everyone looks so shocked. Some people say, "OMG! People actually do this? Don't they feel ashamed of themselves or feel bad?"

Kiana looks at Tanya for one solid minute with a dirty look and then walks away after the assembly is over.

The principal, Mr. Nathan Campbell, summons the three of them into his office and asks, "Why would you do this?"

The trio explains that they wanted to expose the bullies for how mean they truly are.

Mr. Campbell says, "Well, that's not acceptable, and you can't lie to adults. You told the teachers that you were doing a 'Respect the School' presentation—but you didn't. I'm sorry, but I have to notify your parents. You're suspended for three days. Don't say anything else, or you'll get a detention in my office for a full day."

They get picked up and go home. Tanya texts the group chat and says, "Presentation went wrong!"

Jake and Diamond read it and say, "Yeah, we know. We were there."

Jake says, "But, I mean, my parents accept it and said it was the right thing to do. We should get rid of mean people."

Diamond says, "Yeah, my parents accepted it, too. They're not mad that I got suspended."

Jake replies, "Me 2."

Tanya says, "Same."

Tanya puts her phone away, does her usual routine, and is ready to stay at home for a few days.

Bullies Apologize

A few days later, Tanya, Diamond, and Jake return back to school from suspension. They are eating lunch together, and all the bullies come up to them and say, "We are very sorry about bullying everyone. Also, we apologize to all three of you."

They all say, "It's okay! But you should apologize to whoever you bullied, not us."

They all sit together and Carlos says, "We started to bully and do bad things because in Minneapolis, we used to live in the 'hood, which is a gang area. We were trying to fit in and be liked by others. That is why we were acting up. After the three of you exposed us all, we realized that we misunderstood ourselves, and we wanted to apologize to you three and the students we bullied."

It is Riku's turn to say, "Yes, I admit doing bad before, but I am not ashamed. I stole medicine from a pharmacy because I was trying to help my sick grandmother feel better. She is my role model, and I wanted to help even though I didn't have any money. She wasn't feeling good for several weeks. I stole cough syrup, headache medicine, and a blood pressure kit."

Jake is stunned to hear this. He looks down at his feet and says, "I am so sorry for what we put you through. When you talked about why you bullied people, that is when I realized that we should have never, ever exposed you all in a presentation like that."

Diamond then says, "I know what you guys went through because back in middle school, I bullied Tanya. When we were at a family reunion, we actually turned out to be third cousins. And when I found out, I know I had to apologize for bullying her. We are very sorry about making the slideshow. I thought this would help people see how mean you guys are, but we were bullies to you all, too, doing this whole thing."

Last but not least, it is Tanya's turn to apologize. Almost in tears, she says, "I am sorry for exposing Riku and Kiana. I mostly want to apologize to Riku because I did not know he stole all that medicine for his sick grandmother. Next time, I won't be so judgmental. Never judge a book by its cover."

They all say sorry to the bullies and give each other hugs. Ivanna then remembers that the whole ninth grade class is going to have a bonfire next Friday on Bombay Beach from 5:00 p.m. to 10:00 p.m.

Tanya and the other two didn't know about this because they were suspended from school, so Tanya says, "Oh, that's cool. I might come."

Diamond says, "I might go as well."

Jake says, "I'm going for sure!"

When school is over, the three of them hang out together at Tanya's house. It is a Thursday afternoon, so they do their homework, play with Zoozoo for a little while, and talk. Tanya says, "Oh, Jake, I forgot to tell you something."

Diamond then whispers in Tanya's ear and says, "Oh, about the cousin thing?"

Tanya says, "Yeah."

So, Diamond and Tanya say to Jake at the same time, "We are cousins!"

Jake says, "OMG really? How!?"

Diamond explains that her grandma and Tanya's grandma are cousins, so that means she and Tanya are third cousins. Jake says, "Wow . . . no wonder you guys got along really well now. I remember in middle school you two got into fights, had total beefs with each other, and fought over me."

They both say, "Yeah, but we are totally cool now."

Jake says, "Well, I'm glad."

Once the fun is over, everyone goes home and goes to bed thinking about how they are going to have fun at the bonfire tomorrow night.

Bonfire Time

The whole ninth grade doesn't go to school on Friday because whenever there is an event for one of the grades at their school, everyone takes the day off and gets to chill at home. Tanya does her chores, homework, and gets ready to go to the bonfire. She needs to wash her hair because she hasn't washed it in a few days. So, she washes her hair, blow dries it, and straightens it.

Diamond comes over, too, since she wants to straighten her hair and she knows Tanya is going to do it. It is about 5:30 p.m., and both Tanya and Diamond get ready together. They both wear something casual because it is going to be windy and cold. They don't put on that much makeup: They just do foundation, lip gloss, mascara, and under-eye liner.

They both go together to the beach. Once they arrive, they see their friends, people participating in fun games, food being cooked and eaten, among other fun things. They see Jake, too, but once they say their hellos, the three of them split and go their separate ways with their groups of friends.

After the fun is done, everyone comes together in a huge circle and discusses their favorite thing about being a high schooler. They have to use a microphone because the circle is that big—most of the students can't hear what the people are saying. Most of the students agree that they love dances, activities they can do, and school clubs.

It is Tanya's turn, so she says, "This is not my favorite thing about being a high schooler, but my favorite part about this school year is Jake, Diamond, and I becoming really close friends this year."

Diamond and Jake say, "Aww," at the same time. Then, both of them also say together, "Yeah, this was our favorite school year, too, because the three of us are really close friends now."

The three of them have a group hug, and once 10:00 p.m. rolls around, everyone is cleaning up. Half the students head home. The three are just thinking about how much fun they had, and they already plan on doing it all again pretty soon.

The Talk

On Saturday morning after the bonfire, Tanya and Diamond wake up at Tanya's house after having a sleepover. Jake wants to have an important talk with Tanya and Diamond, so they meet up at a nearby park that is walking distance from their homes. They greet each other and sit down.

Jake says, "I brought you guys here because I want to know how you girls have changed over the years and how you became more nice. Diamond, I want to hear from you first. Why did you become a bully in the first place?"

Diamond starts to tear up, but she starts her story by saying, "I was bullied in fifth grade because I have dyslexia. I couldn't read words, and people called me the dumb girl as well as stupid. One time I was learning to write words, and I couldn't understand. I was almost finished, but this mean girl came up to me, ripped my paper, and threw it at me. She started laughing and called me dumb. I started crying. By the time I got to seventh grade, I wanted to be one of the cool kids, so I started bullying people to be popular.

"So, when Tanya came into the eighth grade, I started to be mean to her. I'm so sorry. I should have never done that to you. I just didn't want to be that girl who got bullied, so when summer came along, my mom said, 'Diamond, I think it's time for you to see this.' She showed me a video of people getting bullied, and each of them committed suicide as a result of it. I started crying, and I said to myself that I was one of them—I was one of the bullies. So, I thought, 'I'm going to change for sure now that I'm going into ninth grade.' So . . . that's my story."

Jake says, "OMG, wow. I never knew that. So, Tanya, I realize your Tourette's syndrome is practically gone now. Tell us about how you have been feeling better throughout summer?"

Tanya responds, "Well, I have been going to therapy and making sure to follow the instructions I was given, so I am feeling much better. I have stopped taking my pills, and I have been listening to rain or ocean music, so that helps me go to sleep much faster. I also just pray to God that I feel better, and I really do."

Jake says, "Well, I'm glad to hear this." Then he says, "I have to tell you guys something, too. I am managing my time, meaning that I am keeping up with football and school homework at the same time during summer. I have been practicing football at the sports club in Bloomington, a nearby city, and I have been going to a tutor who teaches me every single subject in school. I have gotten better. I tell my coach that football practice can't work for me every day, but I can go every other day. He says that's fine, so that is how I manage my time now."

The two girls say, "OMG, that's great for you! Both of us are really proud of you."

Jake says, "Thanks! I am proud of you both after our whole discussion."

Diamond wants to hang out with Tanya, but Tanya has to go to one of her older cousin's birthday party. Jake is busy that day as well, so Diamond just stays home.

When Tanya comes back from her cousin's party, she goes to bed at around 2:45 a.m. That party went on for a very long time. She doesn't do her nightly routine because she is tired, and it is very late. Tanya just goes to bed.

Kiana and Tanya Meet

It is a Sunday afternoon, and Tanya gets a text from Kiana saying, "Hey! We should hang out tonight if you are free!"

Tanya is thinking, *Why does she want to hang out with me?* Then she realizes, *Well, Kiana is my cousin, anyway.*

She says to Kiana, "Well, I'm not sure. Let me ask my parents."

Tanya asks her mom, and she says it is okay.

Tanya tells Kiana, "Well, I guess I'm not doing anything. What do you want to do?"

Kiana texts, "Well, we can go out for boba, and we can talk things out about our past. I really want to get along with you."

Tanya says, "Okay then. I love boba, and I want to talk things out with you, too. What time should we go?"

Kiana then writes, "Well, I'm busy until after 5:00. Maybe at 5:30?"

Tanya says, "Sure."

It is about 4:45, so Tanya keeps herself busy by doing her laundry, playing with her dog, doing her homework, and helping her mom. When 5:20 rolls around, Tanya's dad drops her off at this place called Bobalicious, and Kiana is already there.

When she sees Tanya she says, "Hey, how are you?"

Tanya then says, "I'm good. How about you?"

Kiana says, "Doing good."

Kiana's voice becomes serious, and she says, "The reason I brought you here is to say that I am truly sorry for treating you horribly." Kiana tears up and says, "I am sorry for breaking your toys, calling you a spoiled brat, hitting you, and screaming at you. Stuff like that; you know what I mean."

Tanya cries and says, "But why would you want to do this to me? Didn't your parents teach you manners?"

Kiana cries and says, "I never listened to my parents. I don't know. I was stupid back then for doing this stuff." Kiana says again, "I'm truly sorry. Do you forgive me?"

Tanya then says, "Yes."

Both of them cry, and they give each other a big hug.

Tanya says, "Can you make better decisions now?"

Kiana says, "Yes," and both of them start laughing.

Tanya says, "So, to be closer, we need to hang out and talk to each other more."

Kiana says, "I have an idea! Since we have a day off tomorrow, you can spend the night at my place, or I can stay at your place. It doesn't matter. We can hang out tomorrow! Sound fun?"

Tanya says, "Yeah, it does."

Tanya then sees her dad and says, "Oh, my dad's here. I have to go. Do you want a ride back home?"

Kiana says, "Sure. Let me text my parents to let them know I am going with you."

Tanya says, "Okay."

Kiana's parents say that's fine, and they head home. During the car ride, Tanya asks her dad if she can spend the night with Kiana and if they can hang out tomorrow. He says yes, and she asks her mom who also says yes. When they get to Kiana's place, Kiana tells both of her parents about the sleepover, and they say yes. So, they are staying at Kiana's place, and the plan is to have Tanya stay home for a little bit so she can pack her clothes. Both of her parents will pick her up. Once they arrive, they order pizza and boba online, watch scary movies, do arts and crafts, play board games, and have so much fun together. They go to sleep at around 2:30 a.m.

Cousin Bonding

It is a Monday morning of school break, and Tanya and Kiana get ready for their day. They are checking their phones until Kiana tells Tanya, "Oh, yeah! I forgot to tell you that in the afternoon, we are going to Friends & Fun, your absolute favorite theme park! I already bought the tickets."

Tanya says, "OMG, you didn't have to pay for me. I could have told my parents to give me money so I could pay for myself."

Kiana says, "No, no, no, it's totally fine. I know I didn't need to, but I wanted to."

Tanya then says, "Aww, thanks. You're so sweet."

The rest of the morning, they didn't really do anything besides eat, talk to each other, and play on their phones. The afternoon comes by, and they are so excited to go to the theme park. It isn't that big, and people can actually have fun in the small crowd. They go into the theme park, and the first ride they want to ride is Upsiders. It is a roller coaster that has four upside-down loops on it. When they are on the ride, they have a blast. The girls are screaming and having fun. The cool part is that they have an attacher on the front and on the back of the seats where you can record the whole ride on your phone. After the ride is over, they tell each other that they have so much fun on the ride.

They go on two more rides that are not upside-down, and after they go on a snack break. Kiana orders very cheesy nachos with a medium-sized cup of soda, and Tanya orders a corn dog with a medium-sized cup of lemonade. Their dessert is cotton candy. They talk about how they have been getting along much better, how much fun they are having with each other, and many other things. Since they just ate, they decide to wait thirty minutes before boarding rides again. After walking and talking, the girls go back on the rides once the thirty minutes passes.

Kiana's dad is on his way to pick them up. After the last ride, they head out of the park to go home. Kiana and Tanya decide to buy two more bags of cotton candy for themselves. Their cotton candies are pink and blue. Once they arrive home, Tanya's dad comes to pick her up. On the drive home, Tanya's dad asks her, "Did you have fun?"

She says, "I had so much fun, and I would really like to spend more time with Kiana. After this bonding time we shared, I really feel like I am close to her now."

Her dad responds, "That's good. I am glad."

Once they get home, Tanya takes a nap since she is tired from a long day. Once she wakes up, she does her normal routine that she does every single day. Since she took a nap, she stays up for half an hour. When she gets tired, she goes to bed.

The Bullies' Presentation

On that Tuesday morning after brunch, all of the students go to the gym because the bullies have to do a presentation. Tanya decides to sit next to her best friends because she realizes that she hasn't been spending much time with them lately. Once everyone starts to settle down, the students come and talk about why they bullied people, why they were so cruel to people, and last but not least, why they didn't know any better and did things that were not accepted where they previously lived. They don't have anything to present to the whole school, but they just talk about their lives and their pasts during the assembly. It becomes emotional for them, but they speak about it and come through. Once the assembly is over, they make clip-on pins that say, "Stop bullying right now." They want to do the right thing and not the wrong thing. It goes by grade level, so they have four tables with tons of pins. Each grade forms a line and receives one pin before heading off to class.

After school, Tanya gets picked up by both of her parents, and she tells them about how the bullies apologized in front of the whole school and how they made tons of pins to give to each student.

They both say, "Wow, it takes guts to apologize to the entire school, and it's hard work to make that many pins." Then they add on, "But that's good that they also apologized. They did the right thing."

Once they drive back home, Tanya does her normal routine, but this time, guests show up at her house. She talks to the guests for a little bit, then she goes back to her room and drifts off to sleep.

Anti-Bullying Merchandise

In Tanya and Serena's sixth period Leadership class, Mr. Carson introduces Jake's dad, Mr. Mike Bridges, who is the advisor for the class. Mr. Carson talks to the kids about making school merchandise since they don't have any at Bridge Bank High School. The students all agree and think it is a great idea.

A boy named Noah says, "We should put the school mascot on the merchandise. The merchandise could range from sweatshirts, sweatpants, notebooks, stickers, planners, folders, backpacks, and more!" Noah proposes the idea that the school merchandise should also print out anti-bullying slogans on their clothing and supplies. The rest of the students agree and come up with #STOPBULLYING, #AWARENESS, and #THISISNOTRIGHT.

Mr. Carson and other students agree, "For sure, we should do that. Also, maybe in a couple of weeks we should throw a school party. Not at school, but we can rent out a mansion."

Tanya says, "Well, if we create merchandise, we can raise enough money to rent out a mansion because, you know, renting out a mansion is crazy expensive. Let's pitch that and get the principal's approval!"

Everyone says, "Yes, we should do that. It would be super fun."

When brunch comes along, Mr. Carson and other teachers talk about the merchandise idea for a very long time. They go into the office and hold a meeting with the principal to discuss the situation.

Once the students all talk about raising money for anti-bullying campaigns, Mr. Bridges then says, "I will make a deal with the students."

Serena says, "So what's the deal?"

Mr. Bridges explains, "If you all raise enough money and it becomes a successful fundraiser, then I will personally throw a party for all the students and rent a mansion out."

Once their idea got approved, Principal Campbell says on the speakerphone, "Mr. Mike Bridges has personally offered to rent out a mansion and throw an epic party if enough money is raised for the school merchandise and anti-bullying campaign."

The principal and teachers come out of the office and are curious to see what the students think. Most of them think it is a great idea. Some students don't have any interest at all and don't even care about parties. For the rest of the day, Tanya and her classmates don't have anything to do. They can do whatever they want, such as watching a movie. When school is over finally, Tanya consults her mom about the school merchandise. She thinks it is a smart idea and approves of the epic school party in a couple of weeks.

Tanya heads home to get ready, because she needs family time. She wants to eat at a restaurant called Zoku's, which serves Japanese food. They get home late, so Tanya doesn't do her routine. Tanya just drifts off to sleep once she is back home.

The Meeting

On a Friday afternoon during lunch time, Principal Campbell turns on the mic of his loudspeaker and says, "Whoever is interested in making merchandise and whoever wants to go to the epic party, meet in the gymnasium during fifth period. Once the meeting is over, you can head back to class."

He turns off the loudspeaker, and once lunch is over, most of the students are in the gym, including Tanya and her friends, Jake and his friends, and Diamond and her friends. Principal Campbell begins the meeting by giving a presentation on bullying and its negative effects. He shares that one out of every three students in middle school gets bullied, while one out of every four in high school gets bullied. He reminds the students to look out for each other and tells them, "You want to be an upstander and not a bystander." The students agree and nod their heads.

Mr. Carson and other teachers say that next Friday, they can all go somewhere that makes merchandise for their school. The students also have the option to observe the process of creating merchandise. Before everyone leaves to go to fifth period, they hand out field trip flyers to whoever is interested. After that, Tanya goes to sixth period, and then school is over.

Tanya has to go home with Serena because Tanya's parents are busy. When she arrives home, she completes the tasks she has to do for a couple of hours, despite being home alone. Once it is around 6:45 p.m., Tanya's parents come back home, and Tanya prepares dinner. It is just spaghetti and chicken. Once they are eating at the dinner table, Tanya tells them about the fundraiser plan. Her parents think it is a clever idea. Once dinner is over, Tanya completes her usual routine and heads to bed.

Field Trip Time!

It is the day of the field trip. Tanya and other students who attended the meetings are excited for the new experiences, which includes seeing how merchandise is made. The place is called Merchandise and Fun. It is a factory forty-five minutes away that produces clothing and school supplies. The plan is to leave after brunch time with all of their belongings, stay there for a couple of hours to see how everything is made, and finally have the bus drop the kids off back at their homes once the field trip is over.

Once they arrive, the students see four popular YouTubers picking up their own merchandise that was being made. The students are really happy to see their favorite YouTubers that they watch on their smartphones. Some students even get to take a picture with the Internet celebrities. They also see how the workers label the names for T-shirts, sweatshirts, and pants. For lunch, they have a choice of bringing lunch from home or to buy food from Merchandise and Fun's deli. About half of the students bring lunch from home because they think, *Who wants to wait in such a long line just for food?*

Once everyone grabs lunch and sits down, Mrs. Elizabeth Muka—
the art teacher and field trip advisor—announces that in one hour,
they would be seeing how their school merchandise is going to be
made. With their one-hour lunch break, the students have time to
hang out, use the restrooms, and buy more food if they please. Once
one hour goes by, they go to a place where the company makes school
merchandise. When the students are in the room, they witness how
their school's merchandise is made. Everyone is shocked, saying, "Wow,
that's so cool. They're making merchandise for our school."

A few workers explain how it all works and give a rundown on
where they get the time to make all of the merchandise. One worker
asks, "Does anyone have any questions?"

Tanya asks, "How does the school get in contact with you guys to
make our merchandise?"

The worker says, "All you have to do is call our number and tell us
you want to make merchandise. Also, you have to pay the amount of
money it costs for the amount of merchandise you request. One time,
this YouTuber wanted one million shirts for her fans, and she had to
pay one million dollars, because each shirt costs one dollar to make.
It's cheap, but it's actually good quality. It's cheap because we make
good money and lots of famous people with fans or followers come
to us. For example, if a person has one million fans, and they want
to make merchandise for them, they would have to pay one million

dollars because of the amount of fans they have."

Everyone is like, "OMG, wow, that's so cool! But that's crazy expensive at the same time."

The workers say, "That's the drill. If you want to make something, you have to pay for it."

A different worker says, "Another example is if you want to make merchandise for the whole school, you're gonna have to pay that amount of money for all the students in the school."

Everyone agrees that's too expensive. Once the field trip is over, they drop of the kids at their houses. There is traffic, but one teacher named Mr. Thorne announces that it will take weeks to make the merchandise because of the high volume of students there are at the school. Crazy students demand the merchandise right now, but they have to wait.

Once everyone gets home, Tanya's parents ask about how the field trip went. Tanya just talks and talks about it, and once she is done talking, they have dinner. This is Tanya's favorite meal: Veggie burgers. Once she eats dinner, she does her normal routine and goes to bed.

Selling Merchandise

A few weeks pass by, and the merchandise finally comes in! In the gym, there are six helpers for each class of freshman, sophomores, juniors, and seniors. They are going to sell the merchandise during sixth period, so whoever wants merchandise comes to the gym, pays for whatever they want, and goes back to class. Depending on how much money they raise, they are planning to rent out a mansion for the night and throw an epic party in it.

Once they are finished getting everything set up, they wait. A couple of minutes pass by, and lots of students pour in. On the loudspeaker, a staff member says that whoever is a freshman buys merchandise from a certain table. Once she says that, the students already know how this is going to work.

Tanya, Jake, and Diamond are at one table, and each one of their friends sits at a different table. The same goes for sophomores, juniors, and seniors.

Tanya says, "You guys, I really hope we can sell enough merchandise, because I really want this party to happen. And like in a mansion . . . that's crazy!"

Jake says, "I know, same."

Diamond says, "Yep, but trust me, both of you, we will!"

They sell merchandise for almost an hour. Their hands are so tired, and they feel drained. They decide to only sell T-shirts, sweatpants, and hoodies because they think that selling school supply merchandise is too much. Students help count the money. Teachers help count the money, too.

Once they are done counting, the results are in—they raised $18,000! Everyone cheers. They are so excited—not only because they sold that much clothing, but also because they made enough money to rent out a huge mansion in the Hills. The principal reports through the speaker, "Mark your calendars for March 20. We are having an epic party in the Hills!"

The kids yell from their classes, "Yeah, party time! This is going to be epic."

Even in the gym, kids are raving about how exciting this party is going to be. Tanya and her friends are very excited. Once the excitement is over, the school day is over, and everyone heads home. Tanya blabbers on in the car about how much money they raised for the party, and how she and her friends are stoked. She can't wait to tell her mom when she gets home. Her dad thinks that this is a super cool idea.

When they arrive home, Tanya searches for her mom and finds her. Tanya is so excited that she accidentally knocks over a plant, and the pot breaks. She feels really bad and says sorry to both of her parents for being too hyper about this. They both say it is okay, and that she can clean up the mess and tell her mom everything after she calms down. She cleans the mess and sits down with her mom, explaining everything she had told her dad in the car.

Karen says, "Wow, that is a lot of money. I am sure that you will have fun at this party. Tell me the information about it when you and Serena head there."

Tanya replies, "Sure thing."

After getting all hyped up about this, Tanya does her normal routine and goes to bed.

Epic Party Time

It is the day of the party, and Tanya heads to Serena's house to get ready. Tanya is already in her outfit, but over at Serena's house, she brings her straightener to straighten her own hair as well as Serena's hair. The last things she brings is her makeup and swimming suit because she doesn't want to use Serena's makeup. Once they both get ready, Karen calls and asks, "What time are you going to be home?"

Tanya says, "Well, the party starts at 5:00 p.m. and ends at 10:00 p.m."

Karen says, "Okay, then I will wait until you come back home, because I want to see you and talk about how that party went."

Tanya says, "Sure thing!"

Karen asks one more question, "Did you only raise that money to rent out that mansion, or are there any other supplies?"

Tanya says, "Other supplies, too, such as food, drinks, plates, cups, forks, and well, you get the point."

Karen says, "Okay, bye. You have, fun, sweetie. I love you!"

Tanya replies, "Thanks, Mom. I love you, too," and ends the call.

On their way over, Serena's mom asks, "What's the address again? I forgot."

Serena says, "Here, let me set up a Google Maps. The address is 8350 Hill Side Drive."

Serena's mom says, "Thanks!" and starts driving. On their way over, they talk, listen to music, and have fun.

Once they arrive, they see Principal Campbell chaperoning the party and say hello. When they enter in heavy double-glass doors, they experience how big and fancy the mansion is: it is eight thousand square feet with marble floors, fifteen-foot ceilings, very decorative wallpaper, and nice furniture! Serena's mom leaves, and the girls head inside. They see a crowd dancing, eating food, and drinking sparkling cider. They run into their friends, give each other hugs, and decide what to do. Diamond sees Tanya and gives her cousin a big, big hug. They talk about how they haven't seen each other in a long time and how they should hang out someday.

Diamond then sees Jake and says, "Oh, there is Jake! Let's go say hi."

Tanya says, "Okay," but first she tells her friends that she will be right back. They go say hi to Jake, and he gives both of them hugs. Jake says that the three of them should go to the movies and grab boba. They all agree on these plans.

Tanya says, "It was good talking to you both! I have to get back to my friends. They are waiting for me."

Tanya's friends want to play tennis since there is a tennis court. They want to go into the arcade and play games, too. They even have a small bowling alley! Also, they plan on dancing, but that is at the end of the night. Once they are going outside, Tanya sees Kiana and her friends.

Tanya says, "I'll meet you guys out there. I want to say hi to my cousin."

She says hi to Kiana and also to Kiana's squad. They talk about how they are all doing and how they haven't seen each other in a long time. Tanya then says bye and walks to the tennis court. They have lots of fun playing, and eventually they have to leave because other students want to play tennis, too. They leave the tennis courts, and the next thing they do is bowl. They bowl against each other, and Crystal wins.

After that, they don't want to play the machine games, so they take a break and drink mango juice and eat snacks like chips and cookies. They talk about how much fun they are having and post it to their Snapchat stories.

Tanya then mentions, "Oh, I have an idea!"

Julie asks, "What's the idea?"

Tanya then says, "I saw a pool in the backyard, so after digesting our food, we can go swim. I brought my swimming suit." All of them hear the idea and agree to it. Tanya then says, "Yay, awesome!"

After they have digested their food, they change into their swimming suits and jump into the pool. They don't just swim—they play games such as volleyball, Marco Polo, ping-pong, among others. It is

Tanya's group of friends, Jake's friends, Diamond's friends, and Kiana and her friends. Only a certain number of people fit in the pool. No one really wants to go into the pool because they have makeup on and their hair done. The people who were brave enough to go into the pool are savages, because they also did their makeup and their hair.

Tanya says, "You're here to have fun. I mean, you can always do your hair and makeup next time." Everyone agrees with Tanya. They get out of the pool, and music is blasting inside the house. The gang goes inside the house to dry up. Principal Campbell approaches Diamond, Tanya, Jake, and Kiana's group of friends and explains that while he didn't approve of their presentation in the first place, he realized that it was a good example of anti-bullying.

Kiana turns to the trio and says, "Yeah . . . I am glad you three exposed us. When we saw the presentation, we were mad at first, but later on we realized that what we did to other students and you three was wrong and unacceptable."

They go upstairs to put all of their bags in one room so that their belongings are safe. After that, they go downstairs and start dancing. After Jake dries up in the large bathroom, he sees the captain of the varsity football team, who is a junior and the starting quarterback, vaping, which is against school policy. Jake thinks to himself, *should I expose him?* He decides not to, but the thought doesn't leave his mind.

The night is almost over, but the part that means so much to all of them is how they are all getting along by just apologizing, understanding each other, and being close friends.

About the Author

Riyani Patel is a sixteen-year-old sophomore at Ann Sobrato High School in Morgan Hill, California. She is a teen author and storyteller. She wrote her first book, *The Boy Battle*, when she was twelve years old to raise awareness of Tourette's syndrome, a neurological condition she has been diagnosed with since she was seven. Tourette's presents as uncontrollable vocal and motor tics.

As a result, she is a Youth Ambassador for the Tourette's Association of America and educates people about this neurological condition that affects one out of one hundred sixty school kids.

She became a writer because she wants to be a voice of today's generation in addressing topics that affect her peers, like bullying. She, too, was bullied in middle school because of her tics, and therefore likes to help people and to be kind to others.

In her spare time, Riyani likes to hang out with her friends, make TikTok videos, and spend time with her family. Her dream job is to be a Hollywood screenwriter. Share your own stories with Riyani at theterriblebullies@gmail.com.

Literary Legacies

This book is brought to you with the help of the nonprofit Literary Legacies. Founded by author David Chappell, Literary Legacies guides students in grades 3-12 through how to write their own fiction or nonfiction book—page by page. Literary Legacies hopes to inspire youth to find healing, strength, confidence, agency, and purpose through the power of writing. Literary Legacies has published close to ten books with several more on the way. They have inspired tears, laughter, fear, and hope through the amazing characters their students create. If you would like to learn more about this nonprofit, please visit literarylegacies.org.